D0538186

Essex County Council

3013021271548 5

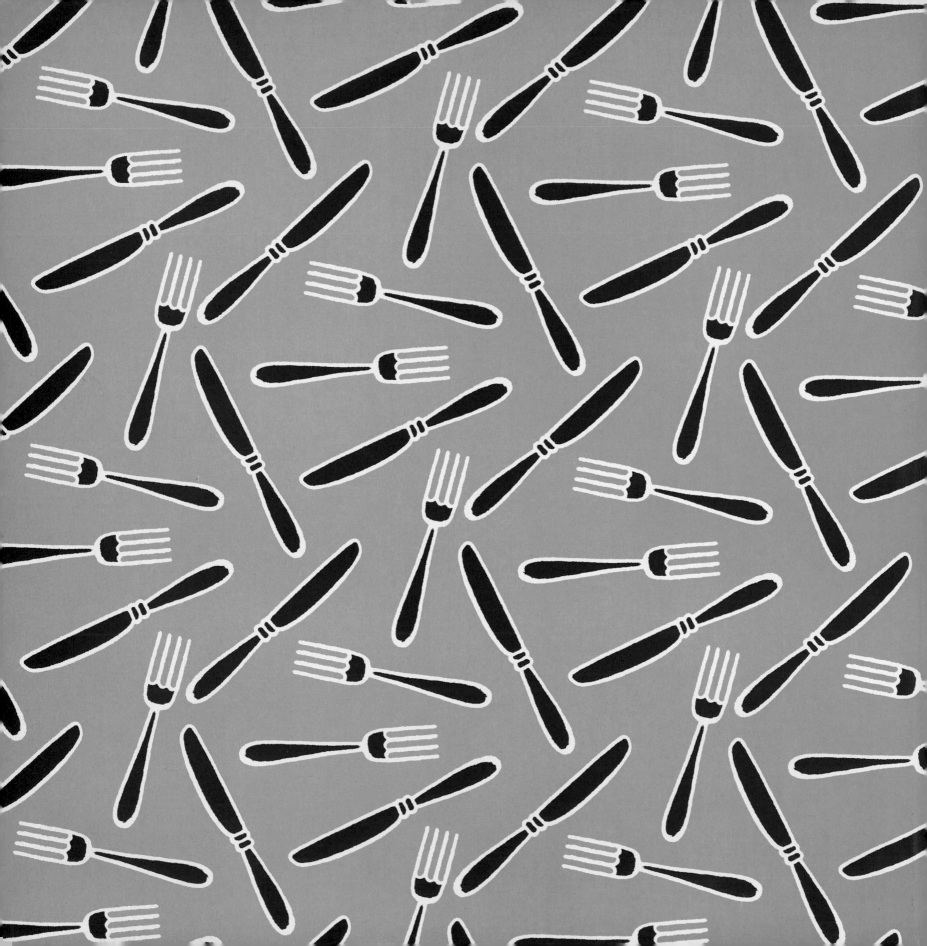

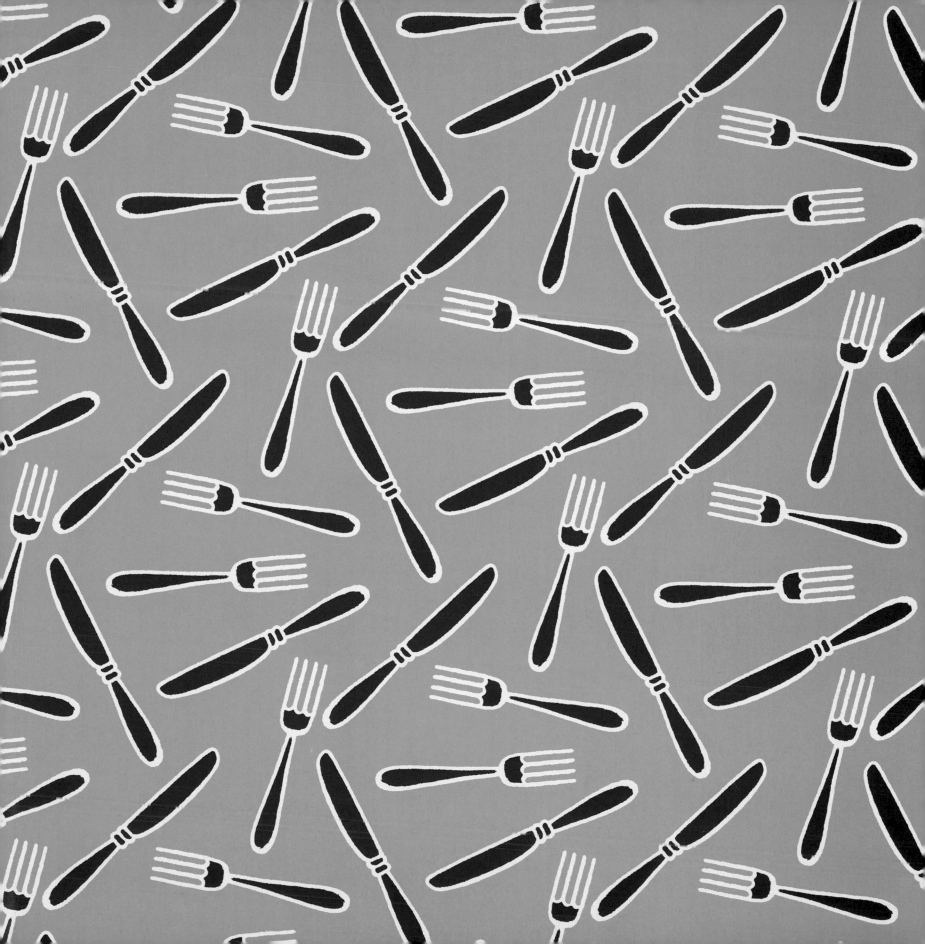

To Claire, Chloe, Kathryn and Rosie – N.G. and E.P.

For Florence – N.S.

First published 2007 by Macmillan Children's Books
This edition published 2016 by Macmillan Children's Books
an imprint of Pan Macmillan
20 New Wharf Road, London N1 9RR
Associated companies throughout the world
www.panmacmillan.com
ISBN: 978-1-5098-1705-4

Text copyright © Neil Goddard 2007
Illustrations copyright © Nick Sharratt 2007, 2016
Moral rights asserted.

The right of Author and Illustrator to be identified
as the author and illustrator of this work has been asserted by them
in accordance with the Copyright, Designs and Patents Act 1988.

All rights reserved. No part of this publication may be reproduced, stored in
a retrieval system, or transmitted in any form, or by any means,
(electronic, mechanical, photocopying, recording or otherwise) without the prior
written permission of the publisher.

1 3 5 7 9 8 6 4 2

A CIP catalogue for this book is available from the British Library.

Printed in China

NEVER use a KNIFE and FORK

Written by **Neil Goddard**

from an original idea by Elizabeth Perry

Illustrated by **Nick Sharratt**

MACMILLAN CHILDREN'S BOOKS

Never use a knife and fork.

Stuff your mouth till you can't talk!

Squish your
fishcake
into gloop.

Use your sleeves to mop it up.

Suck
ice-cream
from
underneath.

Scrape your **biscuit** with your teeth.

Tie your Sausage in a knot.

Paint a picture with your **peas.**

Drink your gravy through a straw.

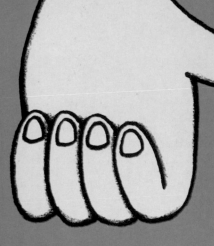

Bung your thumbs in hard-boiled **eggs**.

Pile up **puddings** on your toast.

gave your

dog the

turkey
roast

Juggle **jelly**, tread in **bread**.

But **never**

use a knife and fork!

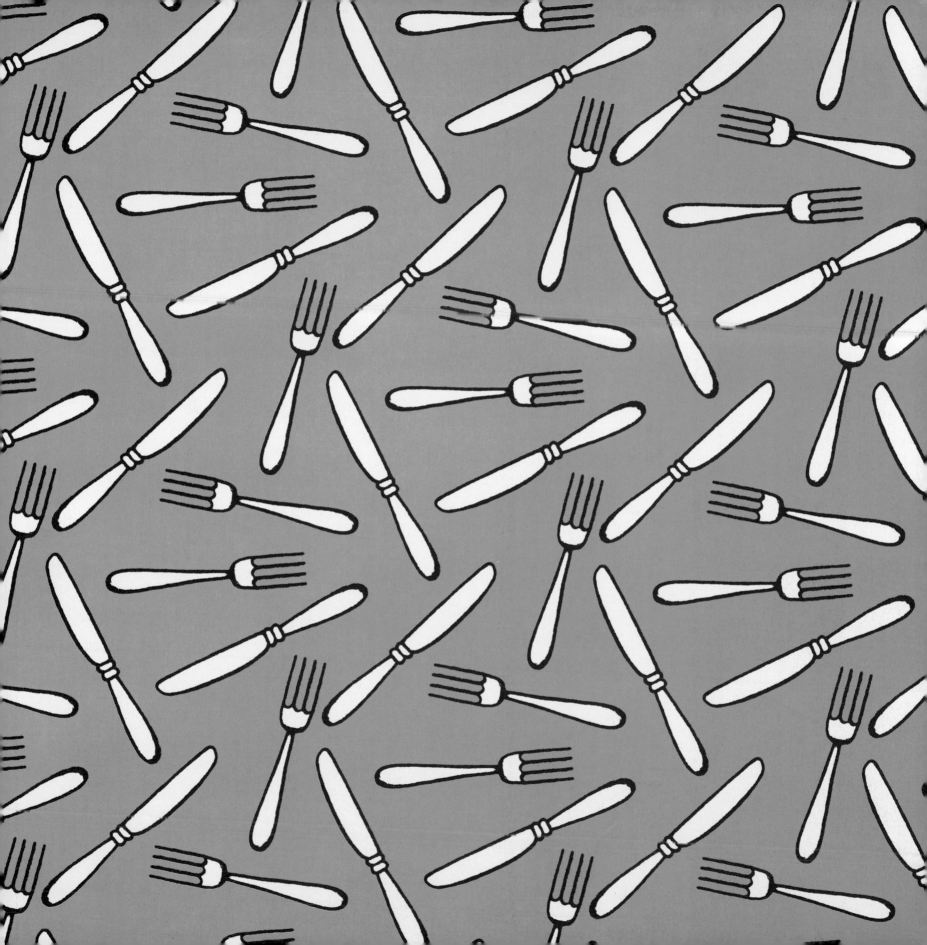

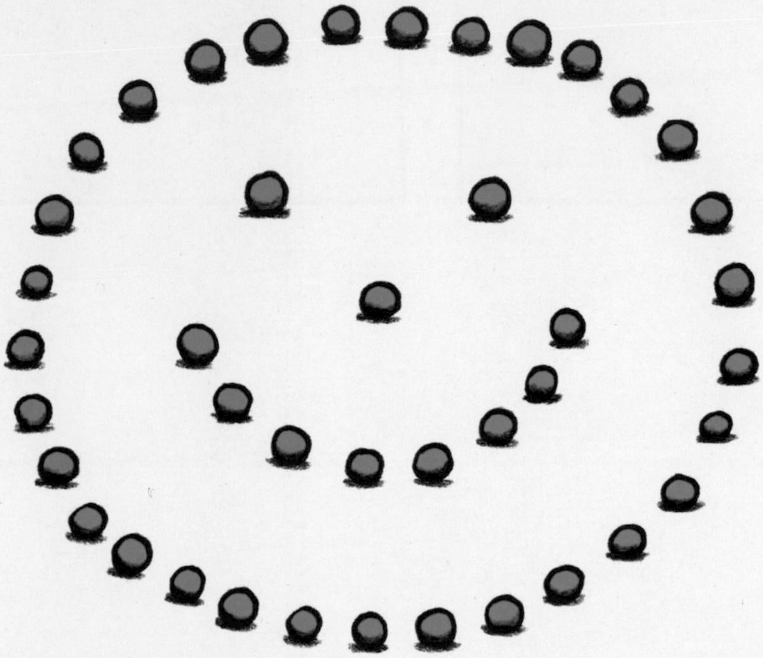